For the children who will grow up and save the world.

First published in 2009 by Simply Read Books
www.simplyreadbooks.com

Text and Illustrations © 2009 Stephen Parlato

Cataloguing in Publication Data:

Parlato, Stephen, 1954-
         Dragons love / Stephen Parlato.

ISBN 978-1-897476-18-5

         I. Title.

PZ7.P23 Dra 2009   j813'.6   C2009-900911-0

Book design by Pablo Mandel / CircularStudio.com
Artwork photographed by John DiCamillo
Special thanks to Betsy and Tom Oursler, and Brian Parlato.

Printed in Singapore

10 9 8 7 6 5 4 3 2 1

Stephen Parlato

DRAGONS LOVE

SIMPLY READ BOOKS

The *World* has not always loved dragons,
but *Dragons* have always loved the world.

Dragons love *flowers*, their colors and perfumes.

Dragons love *butterflies*
that flutter in the sun,
dazzling eyes as they fly,
daylight just begun,

and *moths* most shy
that circle round the moon,
dressed in nightgowns
spun of silk saved from their cocoons.

Dragons love *mushrooms* for their earthy tastes.
They know to choose carefully
the ones they eat...

...lest poison be their *fate.*

Dragons love their cousins the *lizards* and the *snakes*.

Greeting at family reunions they first rattle,

then hiss, kiss, hug and shake.

Dragons love hummingbirds

that dart and dance upon the air,

humming unforgettable tunes
to which they have forgotten all the words.

Dragons love *tropical fish*,

in blues and greens, in yellows and pinks,

coloring their dreams in *vivid inks*.

Dragons love *stained glass*

that glows like dragon fire,

set alight by the sun for all to admire.

Dragons love *scary stories*
in the middle of the night,

reading alone of *skulls* and *bones*
and filling themselves with fright.

Dragons love *birds*
that fill the sky with charm
and do their best to protect them
from those who would do them harm.

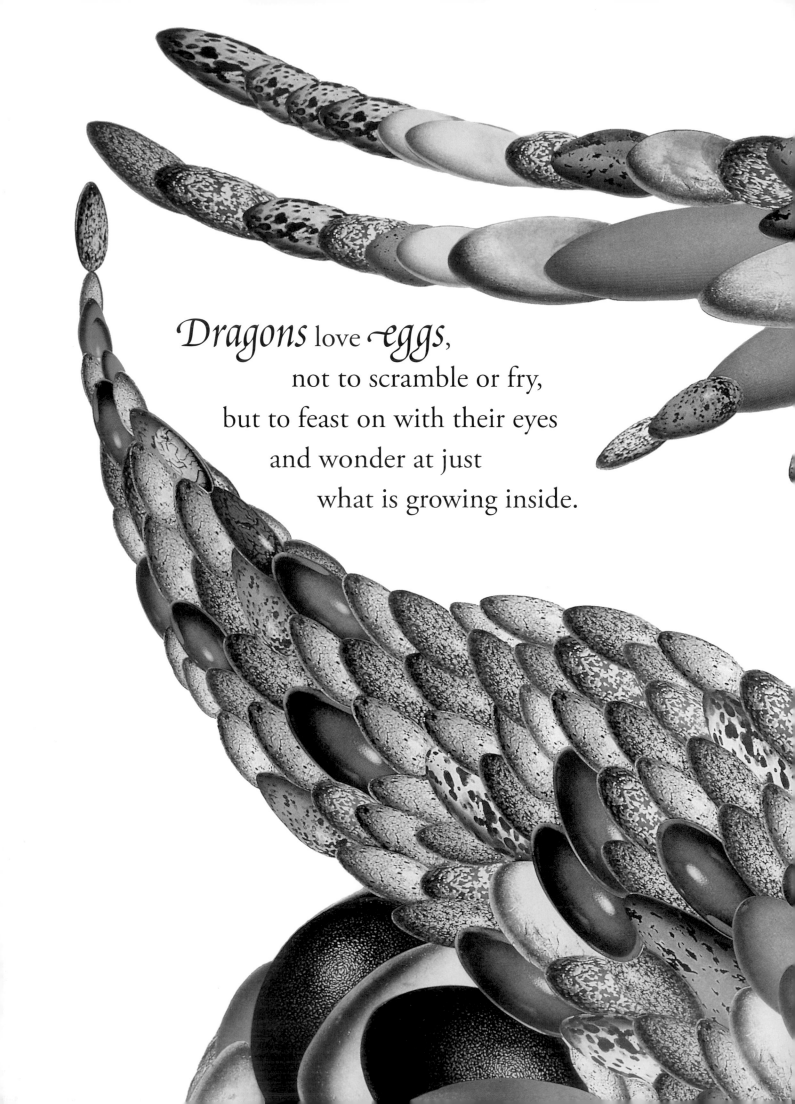

Dragons love *eggs*,
  not to scramble or fry,
but to feast on with their eyes
  and wonder at just
     what is growing inside.

Dragons love *leaves*
that offer summer shade

and then slip from branches to the ground—
wordless poems about the fragile beauty all around.

Dragons love *seashells* that shine and swirl,
gifts to be gathered from the ebbing surf,

reminders of the treasures living below
in the great waters of the Earth.

Dragons love *beetles*

more than the precious stones of rulers,

thinking of them as *living gems*
far beyond the art of jewelers.

Dragons especially love shining *suits of armor*

given to them by brave and chivalrous knights
who came to slay but stayed to *play*
and left a whole lot lighter.

Dragons love *fine fabrics* and *fancy dress.*

Once a year they all meet under the stars at the beach,
where dressed to the nines,
they laugh, dance, mingle and dine,
then boogie on back to their caves.

Dragons love the proud *flags of the world,*

unfurled each day to rise up and wave *welcome*
to all who journey our way
with kindness in their hearts.

Dragons love *books*
that tell *US* stories and also make us wise,
sparking our imaginations,
while sharing the *wonders* of being *alive.*

Dragons love their *treasure*
highly polished so light reflects

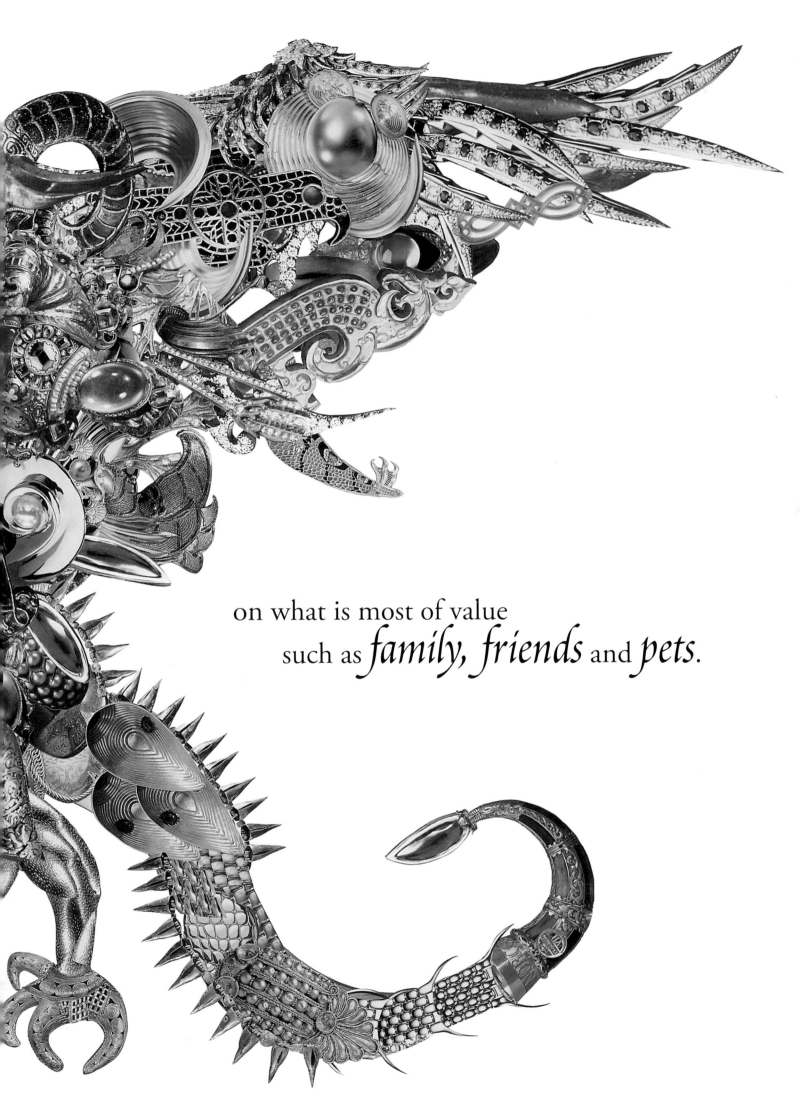

on what is most of value
such as *family, friends* and *pets*.

And what *Dragons* love most of all on this Earth…
…are children like *You*,
who still believe in dragons
and great deeds in great need of doing
and big dreams still worth pursuing.